The Wisdom Circle

The Wisdom Circle

Wade Blevins

Illustrated by
Wade Blevins

Ozark Publishing, Inc.
P.O. Box 389
Redfield, Arkansas 72132

Library of Congress Cataloging-in-Publication Data

Blevins, Wade, 1973-
    The wisdom circle / Wade Blevins ; lllustrated by
Wade Blevins.
        p.   cm. — (Cherokee Indian legend series ; 5)
        Summary: When her favorite uncle calmly
announces that he is dying, Jamie begins to reflect on the
Cherokee wisdom circle of life, death, and birth.
        ISBN 1-56763-075-8 (cloth : alk. paper). — ISBN
1-56763-076-6 (pbk. : alk. paper)
        1. Cherokee Indians—Juvenile fiction.   2. Youths'
writing, American.   [1. Cherokee Indians—Fiction. 2.
Indians of North America—Southern States—Fiction. 3.
Death— Fiction. 4. Youths' writings.] I. Title. II. Series:
Blevins, Wade, 1973- Cherokee Indian legend series ; 5
        PZ7.B61865Wi 1996
        [Fic]—dc20
        96-10302
        CIP
        AC

Ozark Publishing, Inc.
P.O. Box 228
Prairie Grove, AR 72753
Ph: 1-800-321-5671

Printed in the United States of America

ACKNOWLEDGMENT

I would like to thank my 103-year-old great-grandmother, who passed on her knowledge of the past to present and future generations and, in so doing, helped to preserve our Cherokee culture. Maude Parris Gardner, born of a Cherokee father and an English mother, was raised on the Illinois River in Indian Territory, now Oklahoma. Her stories of Cherokee superstitions and her knowledge of wild herbs and plants to be used as medicine and food have provided the family with hours of entertainment. In this age where everyone is attempting to find his or her identity, through her I know who I truly am. Through the efforts of

Native Americans, our culture will remain for our children and our children's children. It is not the color of one's skin, but the content of our heart that denotes a true A NI Y UN WI YA, a Cherokee. WA DO (Thank You).

FOREWORD

Jamie learns a valuable lesson about life from her dying uncle.

The Wisdom Circle

Other books in this series

Jamie sat at the table speechless. It seemed unreal to her that Uncle A-hu-li (Drum) just walked in, fixed a plate of beans, then calmly announced that he was dying. Mealtime for the family, usually so loud and boisterous, became instantly silent. Then all at once, the family erupted into hundreds of questions. All except for the old ones like Granny Wa-ya, who just nodded their heads sadly.

"But what's wrong?" Jamie finally whispered.

Uncle A-hu-li had always been her favorite. Ever since she was a little girl, Uncle A-hu-li had

1

taken special care of her and given her things. Jamie felt that he was the only one who really understood her.

"Nothing is wrong, Wa-na," he said, smiling. He always called her by her Cherokee name. "I've never felt better."

"But I don't understand," Jamie persisted.

"Wa-na, today I saw the Ground Snake."

Jamie heard her mother gasp.

"I don't understand, Uncle A-hu-li."

"The Ground Snake is a great serpent who is colored like the earth. It is an omen of death to

2

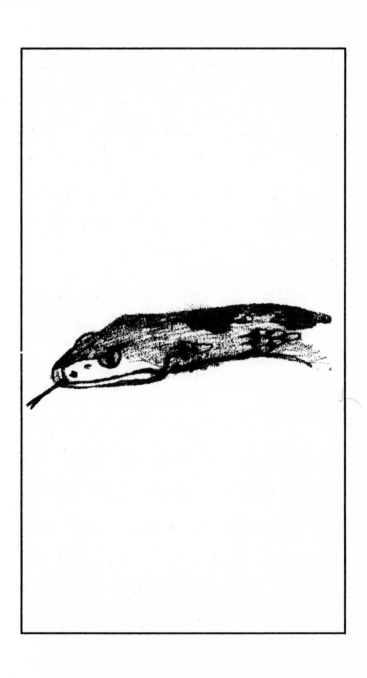

those who see it. Some three hundred Cherokees saw the Ground Snake during a celebration. Three days later, the first group of Cherokees began the long march over the Trail of Tears. The Ground Snake does not lie."

"But the Ground Snake is just a legend, like the Water Cannibals. No one believes in those things anymore."

"You would be surprised at how many still believe. There are still Di-dah-nv-wi-sgi who work for the traditional Cherokees, and many of us still build our houses with the front door facing the East. The more traditional beliefs are respected by

4

most of this family, Wa-na. Now, finish your supper. We can talk about this later, if you want to."

The remainder of the supper was spent in awkward silence.

After the dishes had been cleared away, Uncle A-hu-li and the older members of Jamie's family went out to the Asi, or sweatlodge, to prepare.

The TV and the radio were both turned off, and all those inside began to sing. One would finish a song, then another in the group would begin. The Cherokee words filled the small house, spilling out into the balmy night to blanket the valley like a heavy mist.

All through the night the family sang. Jamie's mother and aunts went into the kitchen at times to fix a small snack or something to drink.

About two in the morning, Jamie fell asleep, her head resting in her mother's lap. Jamie's mother stroked her hair softly and smiled, thinking how big her little girl was getting. She remembered that when Jamie was born, her Uncle A-hu-li asked whether it was a Ka-no-na, a corn pounder, or bow and arrows. When he heard the news, he laughed and said he'd be sure to tell the Wren, who always is happy when a girl is born.

She could remember Jamie running through the house, proudly showing the beaded eelskin hair ties that Uncle A-hu-li had given her. Yes, for some reason, Uncle A-hu-li, the mischievous trickster, had taken an instant liking to young Jamie. His death was going to be hard on her.

About dawn, Uncle A-hu-li came in the door and nodded to Jamie's mother, who gently shook Jamie awake.

"Jamie, Uncle A-hu-li wants you to go with him and the Old Ones to water."

Jamie rubbed her eyes and nodded. She knew that it was a

great honor to accompany him this morning. Silently, she followed him outside. The others were all there, waiting. Together they made their way to the water, each waiting on the bank to greet Grandmother Sun. As the sun's rays first touched the shimmering waves, Uncle A-hu-li entered the water, singing his greeting to the day. Seven times he dipped under, once for each of the seven clans.

Jamie and the others followed, each dipping under seven times. It seemed to Jamie that the wrinkles on the Old Ones suddenly disappeared beneath the

water and the rays of the sun wrapped about their bodies like golden muscles.

Jamie's lips began to slowly turn blue, yet all of her great aunts and her grandfather seemed not to notice, as they laughed and splashed around like children.

Later, Uncle A-hu-li sent for a medicine man to watch him. Calling Jamie over to him, he asked, "Do you know how the earth was made?"

"No, Uncle," replied Jamie.

"When the Creator made the world, it was filled with water. As far as the eye could see, nothing but water. Above the earth was an arch of stone called the Sky Vault, and above that, was Ga-lun-la-ti, the Land Above, where the animals lived.

"Soon Ga-lun-la-ti became too crowded with animals, so the water beetle went to the earth and swam around looking for a place to rest. Finding none, he then dove straight down to the bottom and brought up a bit of mud. Seven times he did this. The small bits of mud began to grow until they created the earth.

"The Creator fastened the earth to the Sky Vault with cords so it would rest on top of the water. Soon the earth began to dry, and the animals sent the Su-li, buzzard, down to find a safe place to live. Now this was the Great Su-li, many times larger than those of today.

"Su-li flew over the earth, but it was still too wet for him to land. He became very tired and flew closer and closer to the earth until his wings touched the ground. Where his wings touched the earth, they made deep valleys, and when they lifted upward, great mountains were formed.

"The animals saw this and became afraid that the whole earth would become one great mountain range, so they called him back.

This is why the region where the Cherokee lived had so many mountains.

"Someday, the Old Ones say that all the people will die, the cords to the Sky Vault will break, and the earth will sink back into the bottom of the ocean. No one knows when this will happen. This is what my grandfathers told me when I was a little boy."

"But Uncle A-hu-li, I don't understand," Jamie protested.

"The point is, Wa-na, that nothing, not even the earth, is forever. Look at these trees around us. To look at them now, we would never imagine that a few months from now these very trees will be bare and in hibernation. It's the same with everything else. Everything must rest, and people are the same. Do you understand now?"

Jamie merely nodded, then ran and hugged him tightly.

"I'll miss you," she whispered.

Uncle A-hu-li hugged her close. He knew that he would miss her, too.

The days passed all too quickly for Jamie. She got up well before dawn and went to the Asi, which had been smoked to keep out A-ni-sgi-na, spirits, and waited for Uncle A-hu-li to come out. They would go to the water and spend the remainder of the day together; Uncle A-hu-li taught Jamie about the Cycle of Life, the Beauty Path, and the Cherokee way.

On one of their outings, they came upon a rattlesnake lying in the warm sun on a rocky ledge. Jamie picked up a large rock, intending to smash it, but Uncle A-hu-li stopped her.

"What would happen if someone took a rock and beat me over the head?" he asked.

"I'd be sad and angry. Then our family would declare a feud against their family," she said angrily.

"Then what makes the rattlesnake family different from ours? Don't you think that they would be sad and angry, too?" So saying, Uncle A-hu-li tipped his hat to the basking rattler, "Brother Rattler, let us not see one another this summer."

Slowly, the rattler slithered off, leaving Jamie staring speechlessly.

"Now he will tell his family that we do not want to see each other this year," stated Uncle A-hu-li. "We will see no more of him or his kin until next spring."

Jamie merely nodded her head, staring in awe at where the rattler had disappeared.

On the fourth day after Uncle A-hu-li's announcement, the medicine man came. He prepared the room where Uncle wanted to die and stayed the rest of the day in the Asi with Jamie's uncle and old family members. Jamie spent the day helping her mother make Ke-nu-che, a dish made of hickory nuts.

Family members had begun arriving the day before to pay their respects.

Later that evening, Uncle A-hu-li asked to speak to the whole family. Everyone gathered in the living room, waiting for him to begin.

"As you know, four days ago I saw the Ground Snake. I've asked the medicine man to sit with me, but he will need a helper. Wa-na, I would like you to be the one. I'll understand if you don't want to."

All eyes were on Jamie, waiting. "Of course, Uncle A-hu-li, I would be honored to sit with you."

He smiled broadly. "That's my girl."

They spent the rest of the night together, talking, laughing, singing, and reliving old times. Even after Jamie grew older, she would always remember that night as one of the happiest in her life. She felt like part of a great circle that protected her and shared her life.

The next morning, the whole family went to water to greet Grandmother Sun and purify the body. Uncle A-hu-li, the medicine man, and Jamie then went to the Asi for prayer and a sharpening of vision.

Afterward, Uncle A-hu-li felt tired and went to lie down, while Jamie went with the medicine man to cut sourwood. The medicine man made four sourwood arrows. The arrows were driven into the ground at the four corners of the house, each one pointing outward. They sat quietly together as the medicine man explained the magic of the arrows.

"By now, the Su-na-yi-e-da-hi, witches, and Ka-la-na A-ye-li-ski, Raven Mockers, know about A-hu-li's vision. We must guard him so that the witches don't eat his liver during the night when their power is the strongest.

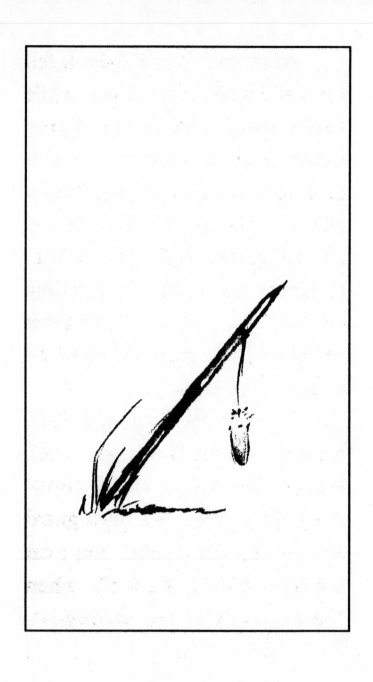

The sourwood arrows have great power over things of darkness and will help prevent the Intruders from entering."

At noon, the medicine man took from his pocket a deer-skin bag containing Tsa-la-ga-yu-li, or old tobacco. He thoughtfully filled his pipe while reciting a prayer to shorten the witches' lives. Carefully, he wrapped the pipe with a black cloth and then disappeared into the forest.

Jamie went back into the room to watch Uncle and to take care of him should he need anything.

The fever engulfed his body just before dark. The medicine

man was outside, blowing the smoke from the lit pipe to the Four Directions. He then came into the room and gave Uncle A-hu-li herbs for the fever. The three talked throughout the night, and Jamie learned much. Shortly before dawn, Uncle A-hu-li called Jamie to his bedside.

He began to speak softly, "Look at this ring. It has no beginning and no end. Life is like this ring. We all make the Circle of Wisdom, each of us drawn forward like a moth to flame. I have nearly reached the point at which I entered the circle, and it is time for me to begin the trip anew.

"I was created from the earth, and now I must return. It is like this for all things in life. What you do and how you affect the earth on this trip is up to you. Always strive to walk the Beauty Path, Wa-na. It makes the trip around the circle something very wonderful. Always keep this in your heart." With that Uncle A-hu-li fell asleep.

Two days later Uncle A-hu-li died. It had been exactly seven days since he had seen the ominous Ground Snake.

Jamie's mother called the nearby church, and the minister began to ring the death toll. The

bell rang for the next hour, signifying that an adult had died.

Just before dark, the people began to come. Family and friends brought enormous amounts of food for those who would sit throughout the night. A death-watch vigil was held to guard against the Soul Stealers until Uncle A-hu-li reached the Darkening Land to begin his new journey.

The house was nearly overflowing with people, all talking and hugging each other. It made Jamie very proud that her Uncle A-hu-li was so well liked.

After all the people had been

fed, the vigil began with a prayer and devotional. Cherokee hymns were sung until dawn. As the first rays of the sun began to appear, Jamie helped her mother and aunts cook breakfast.

That day, Jamie dressed carefully for the service. She rode with her older brother to the small country church, which had already begun to fill with people.

Jamie began thinking of what Uncle A-hu-li had said. Each person who had come to the funeral had been affected positively by him. He had traveled the circle well, and she now understood that he was still here with them. His laughter could be heard in his youngest daughter, and his smile could be seen in his oldest son, David.

David's easy-going smile and mischievous nature had always made the family laugh.

Her uncle's knowledge and philosophy were reflected within herself. Jamie realized that her new-found respect for the traditional ways had come from him.

Jamie smiled to herself and thought that even though Uncle A-hu-li was in the Darkening Land to the West, he still influenced the Wisdom Circle.

The minister's voice inter-
rupted Jamie's thoughts:

"He is not gone, my son
The wind whispers his name
The water remembers his face
His heart has touched ours.
No, he is not gone, my son."

At the end of the service, his
body was carried to the graveside.
The day was bright and airy, and
the hum of locust mingling with the
Cherokee hymns danced together
ever upward.

"Uncle A-hu-li would be
pleased," thought Jamie.

Slowly the casket was low-
ered into the earth, and it was time

to give the final handshake. With
great dignity the minister walked
to where Jamie stood.

"It is the wish of the family
that you have the honor of giving
the first final handshake."

Jamie reached into the
mound of warm Mother Earth and
presented a handful to the East.

"Wa-do, Uncle A-hu-li. I
will always do my best to take
your footsteps around the Wisdom
Circle."

With that she threw the handful of dirt and a circle made of
cedar strips into the grave. This
was her final handshake to Uncle
A-hu-li until they would meet

again in the Darkening Land under the watchful eye of the Creator.

As the other mourners grasped handfuls of the warm earth to give their own final handshakes, a sharp piercing cry from above startled Jamie. She looked up, and there in the vast blue of the sky danced two hawks. They were sailing in an endless circle above the grave. Together they danced in the air around and around the circle. Slowly, something began to descend to the earth. Closer and closer it floated until it came to rest at Jamie's feet. A hawk's feather. Smiling, she raised it in a salute as the two hawks separated with a final cry, one flying to the East and the other to the West.

Jamie knew that this was her uncle's final handshake to her.

That night, the oldest members who still followed the Ancient Ways began the burial dance, which lasted for seven nights.

The next day, the women cleaned Uncle A-hu-li's house, spending the day putting the house in order in the traditional manner. They packed his things away and washed the house from top to bottom, even sweeping the ashes from the hearth.

Jamie was there to take part, keeping a final vigil with her grandmothers. The older women smiled, happy that a young one still took interest.

It was while washing the windows that Jamie's older sister, Quannah, felt her first pains of labor.

Several hours later, Jamie peeked in, "Well, Quannah, is it a Ka-no-na or bow and arrows?"

"Bow and arrows."

"I'll be sure and tell the Wren to protect his shins from the arrows of your son's bow," Jamie laughed. The baby gurgled and smiled A-hu-li's smile.

Jamie proudly carried Sequayah A-hu-li Cornplanter to present him to his family.

Much later, Jamie reflected for many hours on the Wisdom Circle: Life, death, and birth. Each living thing makes its way around, connected to every other living thing, like the earth is connected to the Sky Vault by the four cords.

One's journey completed, he begins in memories, in stories, and in children, making the trip anew until the cords break from the Sky Vault and the earth sinks into the water forever.

"It is good."

GLOSSARY

WA-NA	DAYBREAK
ASI	SWEATLODGE
DI-DAH-NV-WI-SGI	MEDICINE MEN
KA-NO-NA	CORN POUNDER
GA-LUN-LA-TI	LAND ABOVE
SU-LI	BUZZARD
A-NI-SGI-NA	GHOSTS
SU-NA-YI-E-DA-HI	WITCHES
KA-LA-NA-A-YE-LI-SKI	RAVEN MOCKERS
TSA-LA-GA-YU-LI	TOBACCO
KE-NU-CHE	FOOD MADE FROM POUNDED HICKORY NUTS

FOOD

Young pokeweed shoots are cut near the ground, washed carefully, and boiled in at least two waters. The water is drained and the wilted greens are put in a skillet with pork, heated thoroughly, and served with a little vinegar. The root was also dried and used as a purgative, and for rheumatism and skin diseases.

REMEDY

Milkweed juice was used as a healing application for cuts and wounds. Also, the milk is used for removing warts from the skin.

SUPERSTITION

When the Chickadee sings near the house, it means that an absent friend will soon be heard from or that a secret enemy is plotting mischief.